At 9.59 on Thursday morning,
Jodie drew a duck. Top hat, cane
and boots of the softest leather.
On the boots she put silver buttons:
one ... two...

Her pen hovered in the air
for the final button.

To Rosie who drew me the duck

First published 2013 by Walker Books Ltd, 87 Vauxhall Walk, London SE11 5HJ · 10 9 8 7 6 5 4 3 2 1 · Blackbird Pty Ltd © 2013 · The right of Bob Graham to be identified as author/illustrator of this work has been asserted by him in accordance with the Copyright, Designs and Patents Act 1988 · This book has been typeset in Bembo · Printed in China · All rights reserved. No part of this book may be reproduced, transmitted or stored in an information retrieval system in any form or by any means, graphic, electronic or mechanical, including photocopying, taping and recording, without prior written permission from the publisher. · British Library Cataloguing in Publication Data: a catalogue record for this book is available from the British Library ISBN 978-1-4063-4224-6
www.walker.co.uk

Every one of us has the right to experience justice, fairness, freedom and truth in our lives. These important values are our human rights. Amnesty International protects people whose human rights have been taken away, and helps us all to understand our human rights better. Amnesty International has over three million members worldwide. If you would like to find out more about us and human rights education, go to www.amnesty.org.uk or www.amnesty.org.au

Silver Buttons

BOB GRAHAM

WALKER BOOKS
AND SUBSIDIARIES
LONDON • BOSTON • SYDNEY • AUCKLAND

Jodie's brother Jonathan pushed slowly to his feet.

He swayed, he frowned,

he tilted forward ...

and took his first step.

He took that step like he was
going somewhere.

At that moment,
Jonathan's mum played
"Merrily Kiss the Quaker's Wife"
on her tin whistle.

Mum loved the picture of the
wild hare on her calendar so much,
she hadn't changed it in three years.

Outside,
a pigeon nested
under the roof.
As Jonathan took
his first step,
a feather floated
gently past the
window like an
autumn leaf.

Next door,
Alice posted sticks
and stones through
the front gate ...

and an early-morning
jogger puffed on by.

Out in the street, Joseph Pascano avoided the
cracks in the path so the sharks wouldn't get him.

An ambulance shrieked past Jodie's house.

On High Street,
Bernard had his shoelace
tied for the second time
that morning ...

and a man bought fresh bread
from the baker.

One street away, a soldier
said goodbye to his mum.

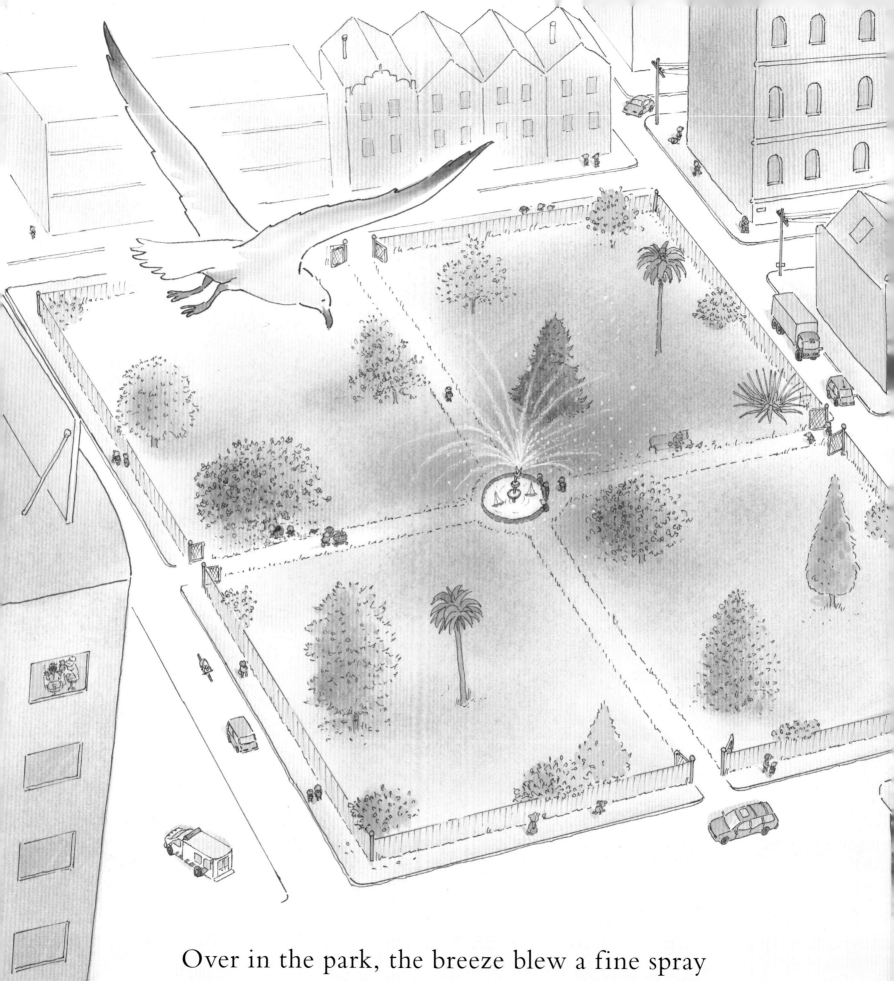

Over in the park, the breeze blew a fine spray
over children sailing boats in the fountain.

Under the oak,
Sophie and her granddad
made a house of leaves.
Sophie sat in the bathroom
while Granddad swept
the bedroom.

On the edge of the path,
a blackbird found a worm ...

and an old lady
carried everything
she had in two
paper bags.

High over the city, a flight of ducks
headed south like an arrow.

In Mercy Hospital, a baby was born.

Over on City Beach,
Belle and Vashti
popped seaweed.

On the shoreline,
Paddy dried off while
Jock scratched his back
in the sand.

Sunlight hit the windows
of the city and phones rang
in a thousand offices
and pockets.

Far out over the bay,
a tanker headed all the way to China.

Then down came Jonathan

on his little pink knees.